THE BIKER'S CURVY VALENTINE

UNDERGROUND CROWS MC BOOK TWO

SADIE KING

LET'S BE BESTIES!

A few times a month I send out an email with new releases, special deals and sneak peeks of what I'm working on. If you want to get on the list I'd love to meet you!

You'll even get a free short and steamy romance when you join.

Sign up here:
www.authorsadieking.com/free

THE BIKER'S CURVY VALENTINE

She wandered in off the street and straight into my heart...

I found her wandering the highway on Valentine's Day, barefoot with torn clothes. She doesn't remember who she is, where she came from, or who gave her the bruises on her body.

I call her Valentine because that's the day she wandered into my life—the day my life changed forever.

Valentine doesn't remember her past, but that doesn't mean she doesn't have one.

And when it comes for her, I'll do whatever it takes to protect my Valentine.

The Biker's Curvy Valentine is an age-gap, amnesia, instalove romance featuring an OTT obsessed ex-military hero and the curvy woman he'll do anything to protect.

Cover designed by Designrans.

www.authorsadieking.com

1
LYLE

Salt air stings my lips, and the wind whips against my cheeks as I speed away from the clubhouse. Gina's decorating for the Valentine's party, and it's the last place I want to be right now.

It seems everyone's finding love apart from me, and I don't need a shitty holiday to remind me of my single status. It's been me and my bike for forty-two years. If I haven't found a woman by now, I doubt I ever will.

As the lines of the highway blur beneath me, my mind clears. It's just me and the road. Just the way I like it.

I lock into a cruising speed, taking it easy and enjoying the scenery, the ocean on one side and orange cliffs on the other. A pickup toots as it passes me, and I give them a friendly wave. When I'm riding wearing my cut, people are either extra friendly on the roads or extra assholey. Today I'm getting all tooting horns and smiles.

I come 'round a bend in the road, and there's a long straight stretch in front of me. Up ahead there's a dark smudge moving along the side of the road, and as I get closer, I make out that it's a person.

Some crazy fucker is walking up the highway. There's no hard shoulder and definitely no footpath. Some fucking idiot is taking their life into their hands.

As I get closer, I see that it's a woman. Her black clothes are dusty and she's barefoot. Something doesn't look right.

I pull over into the narrow sideling in front of her and cut the engine.

"Hey, you okay?"

She doesn't look up as I slide off the bike and start toward her.

The woman's concentrating on her feet, and as I get closer, I see her toes are bloody and covered in dirt.

"Holy shit."

She's wearing black leggings and an oversized shirt, both dusty from the road. Her dark hair hangs limp and tangled, her fringe plastered to her forehead in the heat.

"You okay, sweetheart?"

I stand right in front of the woman, and she stops moving, her eyes taking in my boots and slowly traveling up my body until her gaze lands on my face.

I feel a jolt in my bones as her gaze finds mine. She's beautiful, this lost woman. Bloody and dirty with the face of an angel. Her eyes are deep blue like the ocean, and her thick eyebrows are knit together as she regards me. The dirt of the road is smudged on her cheeks, and there's cracked blood on her temple.

"Did someone hurt you?"

A tremor of rage shakes my body at the thought of

someone laying a finger on this woman. I don't know her, but I feel a surge of protectiveness toward her.

She stares at me, her eyes running over my face in deep concentration.

"Do I know you?" Her voice is croaky, and she coughs after speaking as if the dust has gone right down her throat.

"No, sweetheart. I'd remember you if we'd met before."

Her face scrunches up in frustration, and she turns to stare out at the ocean. I don't understand the emotions running through her, but I do understand one thing: she needs my help.

"What's your name, honey?"

She swallows hard but doesn't answer.

"Where are you headed?" I try again.

But the woman remains looking out at the sea. It's a steep cliff here, and the waves crash relentlessly below us. Her look turns wistful, and for an awful moment, I think she's going to jump.

I grab her arm, making sure she doesn't, and she flinches. Her head ducks and her other arm comes up protectively to cover her head.

The action makes my heart break and my blood boil.

"Did someone hurt you?"

I crouch down so I'm lower than her eye level, less threatening. I know how intimidating I can look with my cut on and my tattoos.

"I'm not going to hurt you, sweetheart. But I'd like to help you if you'll let me."

She drops her arms but keeps looking at her feet.

"My name's Lyle. I'm ex-military," I tell her because that usually softens people's opinions about me. "I'd like to take you somewhere safe where we can get you some food and water and someone can take a look at that cut on your head."

She doesn't say anything, so I push on. I don't want to take her anywhere against her will, but it's clear this woman needs help.

"What's your name, honey?"

She mumbles something that I don't quite catch. I lean forward, and I'm so close her hair tickles my neck. She smells of the road and, underneath that, a sweet scent that's all her. I bet that even if she washed a hundred times, she'd still smell like it.

"I didn't get that. What's your name?"

She tips her head up, and suddenly we're looking into each other's eyes, so close I could kiss her dust covered lips.

"I don't know."

Her voice comes out as a gravelly whisper, and there's a flash of terror and confusion in her face. I'm wondering what the fuck is going on here.

"You don't know your name?"

She shakes her head, her brows sliding together as she looks at her feet. "I don't remember."

She turns her pleading eyes toward me. She's scared and she's vulnerable. I'm fucking angry that no one else has stopped to help her. By the looks of her feet, she's been walking all fucking day, maybe longer. But I'm also relieved that I was the one to find her.

"Okay, sweetheart. I'm going to take you to the clubhouse and get you some help. Is that okay with you?"

She nods slightly and looks relieved, which makes my

chest swell with a protectiveness that I've never felt before. This woman needs my help. She needs my protection.

"You ever been on a bike before?"

She glances behind me to my Harley pulled up on the side of the road. The look of concentration returns to her face, and after a few moments, she shakes her head.

"I don't know."

This woman doesn't know who she is or where she's going. She doesn't even know her own name.

I should take her to the hospital. I should take her to the police. But as she slides onto the back of my bike and her little hands wrap around my waist, she leans her head on my back and gives a little sigh of relief. I know there's no way I'm taking her anywhere but to my clubhouse. Whoever she is, wherever she came from, she's mine now.

2
VALENTINE

My feet throb with pain, and it feels like a hammer is banging on the inside of my skull. I don't know when the last time I ate or drank was, and my mouth's so dry I can barely swallow.

I don't know what came before. All I know is walking. I've been walking on the side of the road for I don't know how long.

I don't know where I'm going, and I don't know where I came from. I just had an instinct inside me that I should keep going, like there's something I need to get away from. But I have no idea what.

My eyelids are heavy with dust, and I close them for a moment. My senses fill with the smell of leather. It's calming. With the vibrations of the bike, I could almost fall asleep.

I cling to the back of the man's bike. Lyle, he called himself. As I cling onto the back of Lyle, I feel like this will be my first new memory, riding down the highway pressed against Lyle's solid back.

It's not long before we're pulling into a compound by the ocean.

I stare at the logo emblazoned on the side of the building —"Underground Crows MC" with a winged skull. I concentrate hard, searching my mind for any recognition, but it comes up blank.

There's a strip club next to the main building with "Girls, Girls, Girls" in neon flashing lights, but we drive past it and park next to a row of motorcycles.

I slide off the bike and wince when my feet hit the concrete. When did my toes get so bloody and raw?

"Let me help you."

Before I can answer, Lyle scoops me up and slides an arm under my legs. My body stiffens, and every instinct is to scream and thrash.

"It's okay." Lyle's reassuring voice cuts through the chaos, calming me down. I'm breathing hard as my eyes meet his.

"Someone really hurt you, huh?"

His look is all concern with anger simmering underneath.

"You're safe here with me."

My ragged breathing slows down, but I still feel uneasy. I'm not sure why my body reacted so violently to his touch.

Lyle carries me through a door that leads to the clubhouse. There's music playing, and red heart balloons decorate the bar. Men in Underground Crows jackets stand around drinking while a group of women sways on the dance floor.

"You found a Valentine!" a big man with a scraggly beard calls out as Lyle brings me through the door. The man's face falls when he gets a good look at me, and I duck my head into Lyle's shoulder, wanting to crawl away and die of embarrassment.

"I need water and some bandages," Lyle calls to his buddies, and there's the setting down of beer bottles and movement as they jump into action.

A woman bustles over, concern written over her features. She peers at me, and her cool hand brushes the hair off my face. Her fingers press gently at my temple, and a pain shoots through me. I can't hide the wince, but I don't miss the look that the woman and Lyle share.

"I'll get the med kit."

"Thanks, Gina."

"What's your name, sweetheart?"

The woman looks kind, and I want to answer her, but I search my brain again and come up blank.

"I don't know." The corner of my eyes sting as I whisper it because I can't even remember the most basic things like what my name is. And things without names are just things. But there's no water left in me to cry.

"Everyone's gotta have a name." I don't like the pity in the woman's look, but she brushes my hair back kindly.

"Valentine," Lyle says decisively. "It's Valentine's Day today. We'll call you Valentine."

For the first time in my new memories, a smile curls my lips upward.

I'm Valentine, and I'm at the Underground Crows MC clubhouse. For the first time in my new memories, I feel safe.

3
LYLE

Upstairs in the clubhouse, we have rooms, so there's always a place to stay for anyone that needs it. They're simple—a bed and chair and a chest of drawers—but it's a safe place for Valentine to rest and recover while I figure out who the fuck she is.

Setting her gently on the chair, I pull up a stool to look at her raw feet. Skin hangs off the underside, and fresh blood seeps through the peeling skin. She must have walked a long way to get them in such bad condition, and she must have a will of steel to keep walking. The pain must be awful.

"How long were you walking."

Valentine's brows knit together in a look that I already know means she's thinking hard.

"I'm not sure. It was dark when I started, just before sunrise."

It's almost sunset now. She's been walking all day in the heat and with bare feet. Anger surges through me. How was this woman left to wander the highway alone like this?

She's dehydrated and her feet are raw, and there's a

purple bruise on her temple. Her body will need time to heal before we can figure out what's going on with her mind.

Gina arrives with a tray full of supplies. I already gave Valentine a few sips of water before she climbed on my bike. I saw dehydration in Afghanistan when I was deployed. There's no doubt that she's suffering from mild symptoms.

I take a bottle of water from the tray and press it to her lips.

"We need to go slow. Just take a few sips."

I hold the back of her head as Valentine presses her lips to the bottle. Her tongue darts out to lick her puckered lips. Even cracked and covered in road dust I can tell they're full. Ripe and kissable.

My dick twitches in my pants, and I silently curse myself for thinking of kissing and more when the poor woman is in such a bad state.

Focus, Lyle, I silently tell myself.

"I'm going to get you in the shower now, wash off this road dust, then we'll get you something to eat."

Valentine nods weakly. She's so exhausted that she's almost asleep. It's tempting to let her drift off now, but I know it'll be better if we can tend to her needs first.

"Come on, darling."

I slide my arms around her and lift her off the chair. I carry her into the bathroom, and Gina follows swiftly behind.

"I don't think so, Lyle."

Gina has her hands firmly on her hips, one eyebrow arching into her forehead.

"I'll help her shower."

She says it firmly, and even though I want to help Valentine all by myself, I know she's right. Valentine's barely conscious. It wouldn't be right for a grisly old man like me to shower her when Gina can do it.

"Go get a chair, then, because she can't stand."

Gina grabs one of the plastic chairs from downstairs and comes back with Lily in tow. Lily is the daughter of our president Bruno and will do anything to help the club.

"No peeking, Lyle," she admonishes me as she firmly shuts the door.

While the women help Valentine shower, I give Bronn a call. I work part time for Sunset Security and he's my boss. The firm is all ex-military men taking private security jobs.

When I explain the situation about Valentine Bronn's understanding.

"Sorry to let you down." I say. "Can you find someone to cover the job next week?"

He had me down for a private job for some oil guy that's getting death threats and wants his wife watched over while he's away.

"I'll do it myself." Bronn says. "Take the time off and look after the woman. Sounds like she needs you."

With the call out of the way I head to the kitchen to look for something to feed Valentine.

The cupboards are full of rice and pasta and a bunch of stuff that I don't know how to make. I was in the Army for twenty years. I never learned how to cook.

At the back of the cupboard are some noodle packets, and I grab those. With boiling water and chicken strips added, I feel pretty pleased with myself.

But before I take the meal upstairs, I have to find Bruno.

The main clubhouse is full of people milling about for the Valentine's Day party. Some have partnered off, but I see Gage and Jesse in the corner playing cards. Two women lean on the bar in short dresses, looking in their direction, but the men are oblivious.

"You'll never find a Valentine playing cards in the corner."

I shake my head at the guys. They're the two serious members of the club, and my comment barely gets a smile.

"You seen Bruno?"

"He's out front with Scarlett," Gage grunts, barely looking up from his hand.

Ever since our boss hooked up with his young fiancée, he spends every spare moment with her. That's why it doesn't surprise me when I find them in a shadowy corner out front canoodling, their drinks abandoned on the table.

I cough loudly, and Bruno gives me an annoyed look as he pulls his lips away from his young fiancée.

"You got a minute, Pres?"

"I'll go check on the girls," Scarlett says, giving us some space. Bruno watches her cross the parking lot into the clubhouse, his eyes scanning the other men at the club, ready to kill anyone who so much as looks at his woman.

It's been fascinating to watch, our President brought to his knees by a woman. But now I understand. The fire I have inside of me burning for Valentine, the protectiveness I feel over her—it's so strong I feel sick.

"Is it about the girl?" Bruno asks.

"Valentine."

He looks surprised. "I thought she couldn't remember her name."

"She can't. That's what I've named her."

I explain the situation as far as I know it. Her bloody feet, her memory loss, the bruising on her temple, and the unsettling feeling that she's running from something.

Bruno listens intently, waiting until I'm finished.

"You want our protection for her?"

"I do."

He nods. "You got it, brother. Anything she needs."

"She needs to stay here to recover. It might take a few weeks."

"She can stay as long as it takes. She need a job? We've got an opening at the club."

He indicates the building next door. The strip club.

"No." It comes out through gritted teeth as jealousy jars my heart. There's no way Valentine is working as a stripper. "She doesn't need a job."

Bruno holds his hands up.

"Alright, brother. Just a suggestion if she needs the work."

His lips pull up in a smile, and his eyes have a knowing twinkle.

"What?" I ask.

"You got it bad, brother."

I stand up, not wanting to admit what he's saying. "I don't know what you mean."

"You will."

He chuckles as I walk away. I know he's right. I've got it bad for Valentine, a woman who I don't know anything about, who could be married already for all I know. But my heart doesn't care. The heart wants what the heart wants.

4
VALENTINE

I wake up in a panic. Blood thunders in my ears, and I sit straight up in bed, gasping for air.

The room is unfamiliar. Red curtains flutter in a sea breeze heavy with salt. The bed is strange, too soft and covered with crisp sheets that wrap around me.

The man leaning over me with a concerned look in his eyes is Lyle. The one thing I recognize. My heart rate starts to steady, and the panic eases out of my stomach.

Then I remember where I am. Lyle fed me soup while Gina bandaged my feet. It was just after she got me out of the shower. Before that, Lyle carried me into the clubhouse because he found me walking on the side of the road.

My mind grasps backwards, looking for more. But no matter how hard I concentrate, there's nothing before the walking. The first thing I remember is waking up on the side of the road in the predawn light and walking.

"You okay?"

Lyle sits on the bed next to me and takes my hand in his. He looks tired, dark circles under his eyes.

"I'm fine." My mouth's dry, and he passes me a glass of water. I drink it all down until Lyle pries the glass off me.

"Take it easy. You're still recovering."

Sun streams in the window. It must be at least midday.

"How long have I been out?"

"Two days."

I can't have heard that properly. That's another two days I've lost.

"I can't have been in bed for two days."

Although that would explain my urgent need to pee.

Lyle nods. "You needed the sleep."

"I need the bathroom."

He smiles as I swing my legs over the edge of the bed, but my body feels heavy, sluggish. Without having to ask, Lyle wraps his arms around my waist and lifts me out of bed.

"You can't walk on those feet for a while."

"You are not carrying me to the bathroom." I'm grateful for his help, but the last thing I want to do is pee in front of Lyle, the sexy older biker who rescued me from the side of the road.

He chuckles. "You must be feeling better if you're sassing me."

"I'm serious, Lyle. I need to keep my dignity."

He sets me down on the closed lid of the toilet. "Don't do anything. I'll get Gina."

A flame of embarrassment shoots up my neck knowing that someone has to help me pee, but I remember Gina too. She's kind and business-like. She could have been a nurse, and maybe by hanging out at an MC club she gets to do a lot of nursing.

It feels like Lyle's gone forever, but it must only be a few moments. I spend the time looking around the plain, tiled bathroom and wondering who the hell I am. I'm no closer to figuring it out when Gina arrives.

She helps me do what I need to do and then Lyle carries me back to bed.

They fuss over me, and I can't say I mind it. Gina applies a salve to my feet and re-wraps the bandages while Lyle spoon-feeds me soup.

Lyle must have pulled the armchair over so it's right next to the bed. Once Gina leaves, he sinks into it, looking exhausted. His clothes are rumpled, and I get the impression he hasn't slept.

"Did you stay there all night?"

He looks at me sideways as if the answer is obvious. "I wanted to be here when you woke up."

He's sweet, Lyle, and I feel safe with him. I'm not sure why that's so important, but I feel something in the back of my mind just out of reach that tells me to get to safety.

"Do you remember anything else?" Lyle asks gently.

I search my brain, and I really want to find something because now that I'm rested, I should be able to remember stuff. But there's a big black hole where my memory should be.

"No." I shake my head. "Sorry."

Lyle's eyes darken. "Don't apologize. Don't ever apologize, Valentine."

I smile at the name he's given me. It's beautiful, poetic. It makes me feel like someone special.

His hand reaches for me, and my breath hitches when I think he's going to touch my cheek, but his hand veers upward to brush the hair on my forehead. I flinch as he touches the bruise on my temple.

"Do you remember how you got this?"

I should remember something like that, how I got a big, mean bruise on the side of my head. But I search my mind, and there's only emptiness.

"No... Sor—" I stop mid-apology when I see his stern look. "I don't remember anything."

This time I search not only my mind but my heart. I should feel fear that I can't remember. I should be upset, terrified for the person that I can't remember, the lost girl. But I don't feel upset. I just feel empty.

"When you woke up, you seemed scared. Do you know why?"

I think about my heart rate, the panic that I can't place. I'm not sure why I woke like that. It seemed like my body's natural response, like there's something to be scared of when I'm awake.

"Was it a bad dream?" Lyle prompts.

I shake my head. "No. I don't think so. I just woke up like that, in a panic."

His hands close over mine, and the heat coming from him is reassuring.

"I have to go now and do some club business."

I don't like the idea of Lyle leaving. He's my safe place, the one thing I'm sure of in my new world.

"You'll be safe here. You're under the protection of the club. Gina and Lily and the other girls will look after you. You need to keep resting."

"Then what happens?" I'm scared of his answer because

already I don't want to leave. I don't want to be cast out into a world where I don't know my place.

Lyle squeezes my hand. "Then we try and find out who you are."

He thinks he's being reassuring, and I give him a small smile because I appreciate his efforts. But the truth is, I'm not sure I want to remember who I am.

There's something in the corner of my mind that I can't reach, but it's dark, I can tell. I should be scared that I've forgotten who I am, but I'm more scared that of what I might remember.

5
LYLE

Later that evening, Gina's making a pot of pasta, and I grab a bowl and fill it for Valentine.

My mind goes back to a conversation I had two days ago with Gina. She told me that when she bathed Valentine there were scars on her back. I'm itching to see them for myself, but I don't want to distress her. If they're old wounds, Valentine may not even know they're there.

But the way she wakes up in a panic and flinches at anyone touching her abruptly has me brooding. I need to find out who she is so I can find out if someone needs to pay for hurting her.

I take the pasta into the room where Valentine is propped up on the bed reading a well-thumbed romance book.

"Hey." She smiles when I come in the door, and I almost drop my pasta. She was pretty when I picked her up off the road covered in dust. But with the health restored to her rosy cheeks and her lips healing, her hair washed and brushed, she looks beautiful.

"Hey."

I set the tray down on the bed and resist the urge to kiss her.

"I brought dinner."

She gives me a thankful smile. "Thanks, Lyle. For everything."

She's thanked me a hundred times, but she doesn't know I'll look after her for the rest of her days if I can.

"I've got a game we can play."

Her eyes perk up. "I like games."

I give her a raised eyebrow because that's exactly the point of the game. Valentine has lost her memory, but she can still speak and read and function like an adult. I've spent the day researching memory loss and amnesia. It seems that in Valentine's case it's a certain part of the brain that stores her long-term memories that's affected. She might not remember her name or where she lives, but we can still get to know each other.

"It's a getting-to-know-you game."

She gives me a wary look. "I might not be too good at it."

"We'll see."

While Valentine eats her pasta, I pull out a deck of cards that I found at the local game shop.

"I'm going to ask you a question, and you answer truthfully."

"Okay," she says between mouthfuls. "I'll try."

I pull the first card from the pack.

"What's your favorite season."

"Winter."

I'm surprised by her quick answer and the certainty in

her voice. She looks at me with wide eyes, just as surprised as I am.

"Oh my god. I don't know how I know that."

She gets that concentrating look on her face, and I know she's scanning her brain for a memory, looking for a reason why she prefers winter over any other season. After a few moments she shakes her head. "No. I don't know why, but I prefer winter."

I pull the next card out of the pack.

"If you could live in any country, where would you live and why?"

"Italy. For the artwork."

A surprised look crosses Valentine's face, and I feel it too. She might not remember her past, but she knows her preferences.

"I think I like painting!" she squeals. "Or at least looking at paintings."

She bounces up and down excitedly, and I rescue the half-full pasta bowl.

This is going better than I expected. I just hope it triggers some real memories for her.

"Hold on." I race downstairs because I'm sure I've seen an old art book around somewhere.

Gage is reading in the corner, and he looks up as I jog up to him, pushing his spectacles down his nose.

"You got a book on art? Italian art?"

"Renaissance or modern?"

I have no idea what he's asking me, but the fact that he has both doesn't surprise me. "I dunno. Give me what you've got."

We're probably the only MC in the states that has a

bookcase. Gage sneaked it into the back office a few years ago.

He's our club secretary, and this is his domain. Alongside a filing cabinet, there's a bookcase and a comfy armchair in the corner with a reading lamp. I get the feeling that when he says he's in here doing the accounts, half the time he's getting in some quiet reading time.

He bends down and runs his finger over the spines off the books, touching each one reverently as if he's polishing gold or something. I hop on my feet impatiently.

"Anytime this year will do..."

Gage ignores my impatience and pulls two hefty-looking books off the shelf and hands them to me.

"That first one's..."

But I don't hear what he has to say because I'm already out the door and up the stairs. I throw the books down in front of Valentine, and she picks up the one on top. It's got old-looking paintings on the cover, and even a philistine like me recognizes the Mona Lisa.

Valentine flicks through the pages until she comes to a page covered in glossy, colored pictures, her hands smoothing down the page reverently.

"This one's Leonardo Di Vinci, the *Madonna of the Rocks*." Her eyes meet mine excitedly. "And this one's the *Annunciation*." I lean over to read the text underneath, and she's got it right on both counts.

Valentine turns the page and points to another picture. "This is *Madonna with John the Baptist*. And this one's Raphael's *Transfiguration*."

With each page, her voice gets more excited, and I'm

right there with her. She may not remember her name, but she remembers every goddam picture in that book.

Until she turns the page to a picture of a dragon with a man thrusting his spear into its head. Her brow furrows. "I don't know that one."

The next picture is a woman on a clam shell with her hair wrapped over her shoulder. I've seen this before, but Valentine's face screws up.

"Nor this one."

She doesn't know the next few pictures. They're from old mythology. A man who's half-goat plays the horn, and in another one, sprites dance around a tree.

We turn the page again, and it's a Christian religious scene. Valentine smiles, naming the painting.

She's so pleased with herself. She hasn't noticed she only knows the religious paintings and not the ones from Greek mythology, like those are the only ones she's been exposed to.

I don't have time to think about it because I'm too caught up in the excitement of a little piece of the puzzle fitting in.

"I know this one!" Valentine practically shrieks.

I lean in to look, and we're both laughing, our heads almost touching. I love the way her eyes dance with laughter, her whole face lighting up with excitement. She looks up and catches me looking at her.

We stare at each other, and I can't resist any longer. My lips capture hers, and she sighs slightly as her mouth moves with mine.

She tastes of sweetness and fresh herbs and the salve

that Gina gave her for her lips. I'm gentle with her cracked lips, tenderly exploring her mouth.

My hand snakes around her head to pull her toward me, wanting more, wanting all of her.

But there's a warning going off in my mind. This isn't right. This isn't the time. We still don't know who she is. She's still hurting and vulnerable and so young. She's under my protection, and I won't take advantage of her.

With great reluctance, I pull back.

Valentine's eyes flicker open, and disappointment etches into her features.

"I'm sorry." And I really am. "But I won't take advantage of you."

Her mouth turns down, and I hate that I'm making her frown. "It's not taking advantage if it's what I want."

I stand up and run a hand through my hair, needing to put some distance between us before I do something she'll regret.

"You're here under my protection, Valentine. I won't take advantage of a young woman I'm supposed to be looking after. We don't even know who you are. You might already be someone's old lady."

The thought of Valentine being with someone else makes me shudder, but it's a truth I might have to face.

She sticks her chin out, and there's a fire in her eyes that I haven't seen before.

"Then let's find out who I am."

It's the first time she's mentioned finding her identity, and I hate the shudder of foreboding that goes through me. It's selfish to want Valentine all to myself. Of course she wants to find out who she is and where she came from. I just hoped I'd have more time with her.

But if that's what she wants, that's what I'll do.

"If you're ready, I'll make some enquiries."

I've already checked the missing persons reports, and no one matching her description has been reported missing. I didn't want to put my own feelers out until I knew it was what she wanted.

"I'm ready."

Of course it's what she wants. She wants to know who she is, where she came from.

"I'll see what I can find out."

I leave her in the room with the art books. I should be happy to help Valentine, but all I feel is my own selfish disappointment because I don't want to give Valentine up.

6
VALENTINE

It's a few days since I first played the getting-to-know-you game with Lyle. We've played it every day since, and we've gone through the whole pack and invented questions of our own. I made Lyle answer the questions too. I like finding out about him, and he can always answer the questions with more detail than I can.

Like how he loves winter, too, because summer only reminds him of the years he spent in the Afghanistan desert.

I've learned he's ex-military and has no family, but the MC are his brothers as are his ex-army buddies who he works with. He does part time security, but he loves to ride, which is how he got involved in the club.

I've learned a few things about myself too. My favorite color is amber, and his is blue. I prefer cookies over cake. I don't think I play any sports, which you can tell by my round belly and total lack of muscles anywhere.

Despite loving winter, I don't think I've ever been to the mountains. I don't think I've traveled outside the US and maybe not anywhere outside the state. I can't be sure because I still can't remember, but any questions about geography pulled up blanks.

My feet are slowly healing, and I'm able to hobble around without opening any fresh wounds. I've been helping Gina in the kitchen because it turns out I can cook. It surprised her as much as me when I grabbed an onion and sliced it with the speed of a master chef.

I cooked a vegetable soup for the club and even baked fresh homemade bread.

Maybe I was a cook or chef in my past life. I've stopped trying to remember because every time I do, it comes up blank.

I'm sitting in the clubhouse with my feet up on a chair. I've gotten to know some of the guys over the last few days. Jesse and Gage are respectful and kind, and we've played cards together.

Bruno is gruff but tender toward his fiancée. Kray makes me laugh, and Quinn mopes about always talking about his law student girlfriend. Then there's Pans who I've barely spoken to because he scares the heck out of me. Lyle says he's loyal, which is good because I get the feeling you wouldn't want to get on the wrong side of Pans.

The guys are respectful, and the women are kind, but there's a new emptiness in my chest whenever Lyle's not around.

He hasn't tried to kiss me again. He's kept a respectful distance. I know it makes sense. He's so much older than me, and he doesn't know where I've come from. But the more time I spend with Lyle, the more I want to feel his lips on me. I get it. I might be married for all he knows, but there's no ring mark on my finger, so I doubt that's the case.

Lyle has put feelers out, spoken to local businesses and shown my photo to diners and other places up the coast.

So far, no one has come to claim me. No one recognizes me, and there's no missing person search out for me. It seems no one misses me at all.

The sound of a bike has my head jerking up, but it's one of the other guys returning. I try to hide my disappointment that it's not Lyle.

It's been about a week since he rescued me, and I still feel tired. He will probably scold me if he catches me downstairs. Even though I've got my feet up on a chair, he thinks I should be on bed rest for another week.

He's been looking after me so well that I don't want to let him down. If he thinks I need bedrest, then that's what I'll do.

"I'm going up," I tell Gina as I hobble past the kitchen. I can get around on my own these days and shower by myself, which is exactly what I do when I get to my room.

I sit on the plastic chair to unwrap my bandages while I wait for the water to heat up. The hot water will sting, but the wounds need cleaning.

When someone comes for me, I don't want to be damaged. I want to be whole.

It's a weird place to be, waiting for someone to come and claim you.

As the water rushes over me, I wonder what kind of life I had. Was it as simple and happy as the last week? Cooking and playing cards and talking with Lyle?

But I have a fear inside of me. How good could my life have been if I've not even been missed?

7
LYLE

I grip my handlebars tight as I pull into the clubhouse grounds. It's been another frustrating day of looking for clues about Valentine. I've stopped at every diner within a hundred-mile radius and no one recognizes her picture.

I've had Seth, my old military buddy who does cyber security, help me out. But he can't find anyone looking for a missing woman on his dubious online networks.

I'm frustrated for Valentine, but there's a selfish part of me that feels relieved. The more time I spend with her, the less I want to give her back.

Knowing she's got some other life out there waiting for her drives me crazy, like the happy times from the last week could come crashing down on us at any time. My time with her is limited, and I have to make the most of it.

After I found out her favorite flowers are dahlias, I stopped on the way home and picked up a bunch. I grab them from the back of the bike and head inside.

I take the stairs two at a time, anxious to see her. When I

knock on the door, there's no response, so I push it open slowly in case she's asleep.

The room is empty, her clothes strewn across the bed. It's becoming more like her room the longer she stays. I set the flowers down on the bedside table and am about to leave when the door to the bathroom opens.

Steam billows into the room, surrounding the vision that is Valentine wet and glistening and wrapped in nothing but a towel. Wet hair is plastered to her shoulders, and water trickles down her neck and between her breasts.

She looks startled to see me. Her eyes go wide, and her mouth pops open, making her look sexy as hell.

"I didn't know you were here..." She stares at me but doesn't make any move to retreat.

I should leave, but I'm transfixed. Her skin is dewy from the shower, and she smells fresh, like flowers and all things good.

The urge to stride across the room and pull her toward me is so strong I have to dig my hands into my pockets.

"Sorry, I'll go."

"No." She steps fully out of the bathroom and lets the towel fall. It glides slowly down her body, revealing her soft breasts, the nipples perky and hard. The towel catches on her wide hips and slowly slips down to reveal her downy dark mound of hair.

She's perfect. Completely fucking perfect. And even though my mind is screaming that I shouldn't do this, my body takes over.

Blood thunders in my ears as it rushes to my dick. I stride over to Valentine, closing the distance between us.

My hands slide around her hips as my mouth presses to hers.

She's soft against me, and it's nearly my undoing the way her body folds against mine.

Her hands slide my cut off and pull at my shirt until my bare chest presses against hers. I walk her backwards, back into the bathroom, and lift her up onto the counter.

My heart thunders in my chest, beating for her, overwhelming me with my need for her, my need to show this vulnerable woman tenderness and to treat her body with the reverence she deserves.

My mouth runs down her throat and over her breasts, taking one hard nipple at a time between my teeth. She arches her back and moans as her hands tangle in my hair.

I can't claim her until I know she's not sworn to someone else, but I sure as hell can show her some tenderness, just a little taste...

My hands spread her thighs, and she glistens, wet, her pink lips peeking out through her dark hair. Dropping to my knees, I spread her thighs, needing to taste her, to suck on that sweetness, to give her one good memory.

Valentine tastes as good as I've imagined she would, her freshly washed skin combined with her tangy arousal. She moans as I lick her, taking my time to be gentle. I don't know where this woman came from, but I know she needs some tenderness in her life. I kiss and suck and lick until she's bucking against me, coming on my tongue and filling my mouth with her sweet nectar.

When she's had her release, I lick her again, bringing my cock out to fist as she writhes against me. She cries my name and pulls my hair as she comes, and I let myself go, shooting my cum onto her thighs as she convulses around me.

My seed coats her skin, and I don't care if someone comes for her now. There's no way I'm giving her up.

Valentine's breathing hard, her eyes dreamy from the double orgasm.

I stand up and slide my hands up her back to help her off the counter. My fingers roll over hard skin, and I freeze.

"What's wrong?" she asks.

"Turn around, honey." My voice is clipped, and my arousal instantly turns to anger.

She slides off the counter and turns, and for the first time, I get a look at the scarring Gina told me about.

Vicious lines crisscross her back, the skin puckered in angry ridges.

"Who did this to you?"

The anger in my voice must frighten her because she whimpers and backs away from me.

"What do you mean?"

She's frightened, and I don't blame her. I've gone from relaxed to ready to kill someone in about ten seconds flat.

"I'm not angry at you, Valentine. Did you know there are scars on your back?"

She looks confused, and I realize she doesn't even know they're there.

There's a wall mirror in the bathroom, and I find a small mirror in the cabinet and hold it behind her. She gasps when she sees the scars in the mirror. Her hand reaches behind her, and she can just trace one of them.

Her eyes are wide and confused.

"I don't remember."

There's fear in her voice, and my heart goes out to her. My lost Valentine. There's cruelty in her past, and a new wave of protectiveness surges through me.

I pull her toward me.

"I'll never let anyone hurt you again. I promise."

She's trembling, and I lead her over to the bed. We get under the covers, and I pull her close, wrapping her in my arms.

Her body's spent for today, and I don't demand any more of her. With gentle kisses, I calm her down. Eventually, she falls asleep.

But I lie awake, my furious heart thumping angrily. Someone hurt my Valentine, and when I find them, they'll pay.

8
VALENTINE

For the first time since I woke up on the side of the road a week ago, I wake up without the panicked feeling. Lyle's arm is draped over me, and I feel safe. I feel content.

It was a shock to find the scars on my back last night. They're healed over and faded at least a few years old. It looks like something lashed against my skin, like a whip, and the implications of how I might have got them make me shudder.

Lyle stirs, and I turn toward him and burrow into his chest, needing to get as close to him as I can.

"Morning, beautiful."

I look up at his smiling eyes, and a surge of happiness goes through me. Lyle's smile makes him look younger. I don't know how old I am, but we decided I'm probably about twenty. Lyle is forty-two, but I don't mind the age difference. It makes me feel safe having an older ex-military man by my side.

I wonder what he'll look like in ten years, with our kids

crawling on top of him. The thought makes me smile, thinking about a future when I don't even know my past.

"What's the smile for?" Lyle asks.

"I'm happy," I say simply.

"You want to go out today and get some breakfast? Go for a ride down the coast?"

I've been stuck at the MC club for the last week as my body healed and because Lyle wanted to make sure I was safe. If he thinks it's time to venture out, then he must be sure no one's looking for me.

The thought should make me sad, but it makes me feel relieved.

"Sure. I could go for some blueberry pancakes."

We're talking about what we'll have for breakfast when there's a knock at the door.

"Give me a minute," Lyle calls out grumpily.

"Stay here." He swings his feet over the side the bed. The covers slide down my chest, exposing my breasts. Lyle grabs a nipple in his mouth, making my body arch into him. He lets out a groan but releases my nipple and pulls the sheets up to my neck.

"And cover up," he says, making a show of tucking me in, which makes me laugh.

He pulls his clothes on and is tucking his t-shirt into his jeans as he opens the door.

Jesse is at the door, and one look at his face makes me feel uneasy.

"There's a man here for Valentine."

My body goes rigid, and a chill runs through me. Someone came for me.

"Says he's your fiancé."

The word lands in the air like a lead balloon. My chest feels heavy as my gaze meets Lyle's. Everything that we shared flows between us in that look. The soul-soothing kisses, his tongue on me last night, the future for us I'd imagined in my head.

Lyle breaks the gaze, and all our might-have-beens go crashing to the ground.

"I've got a fiancé?"

The word sounds wrong in my mouth. I search my mind, willing the memories to come back, but it's a big blank.

"I guess you do." Lyle's voice sounds clipped, and he doesn't look at me as he pulls on his cut.

I want him to come back to bed. I want him to kiss me the way he did last night. I want him to take me out for blueberry pancakes.

"You better get dressed, sweetheart."

In a daze, I slide out of bed and put my clothes on. They're not even my clothes. They're ones that Lily found for me and said I could keep.

I wonder if I've got a wardrobe full of clothes somewhere, lines of shoes and folded socks waiting for me.

Lyle leaves me alone to get dressed. I take my time, straightening the bed covers and pulling the curtains, stalling for time and making sure every detail of this happy place is etched into my memories.

It wasn't much, but I felt safe here. I rested and recovered and found friends here. But I knew it was only temporary. I knew I'd have to go back to my real life sometime.

Taking a deep breath, I pull open the door.

Lyle's waiting for me with a smile that doesn't meet his eyes.

"Let's go find out who you really are."

He says it too cheerfully, like he's trying to be excited for me. But all I feel is a dread that gets heavier with every step we take downstairs.

9
LYLE

My hand rests on the small of Valentine's back as we head downstairs. I can feel the ridges of her scars through the thin cotton of her shirt.

There better be a good explanation for how she got those scars. Fiancé or not, if he's hurt Valentine, then he's going to pay.

We head outside where a man in a flannel and dark jeans leans casually against the side of a pickup truck. His greasy hair hangs to one side and he's chewing on a toothpick, the stalk poking out of the side of his mouth.

He smiles widely when he sees Valentine. His eyes dart over her body in an appraising look that makes my blood boil.

"I've been looking all over for you, Abigail."

Abigail. I roll the name over in my mind, but it doesn't suit the quiet and sweet woman I've gotten to know. I keep my hand on Valentine's back, watching her closely.

At the foreign sounding name, her face scrunches up in

confusion, and I guess she's looking for the memories the name and the man might trigger.

"Well, aren't you gonna come on over here and give me a hug?"

He opens his arms, and Valentine steps forward hesitantly.

"Come on then, girl. We got some catching up to do."

She looks back at me, then back at the man, confusion written all over her face. I want to pull her back to me. I want to hold onto her and never let her go. But if this is her past, then I need to give her a chance to find out who she is.

"I bought you some flowers."

He reaches into the cab and pulls out a bunch of gas station flowers. The stems are wilted, and there's not a dahlia in sight. Surely her fiancé would know to bring her favorite flowers.

"Well, come on, then. The wedding's next week, and everyone's been going crazy with worry."

He gives a wide smile and takes a step toward her.

"I don't remember," Valentine whispers. And I hear the frustration in her voice.

"It don't matter, honey. We'll go back to the house and it'll all come back to you."

He takes a step forward. Valentine takes a step back. She swallows nervously, and a vein in her neck pulses. The old fear is coming back, I can sense it in her.

"How'd she get those scars on her back?"

I step forward so I'm between the man and Valentine. The man smiles at me warily.

"Abigail's had those scars ever since I knew her. She

came from a foster family." He looks down at his hands and fists them in a show of anger.

"One of those families didn't treat her so good. It's a blessing she can't remember."

It could be true. The scars look to be several years old. She was probably fourteen or so when she got them. But something doesn't feel right about this guy.

"How about the bump on her head?"

He blinks quickly, and his smiling masks drops for an instant—but only an instant.

"Must have been in the accident. We had an accident last Monday night out on the coastal highway. I was knocked unconscious and woke up in the hospital two days later. By that point, no one knew where Abigail had gone. She must have been thrown from the car. I been going sick with worry looking for her."

As he talks, the toothpick goes up and down in his mouth, giving him a casualness that I don't like. If I lost Valentine in an accident, I wouldn't sleep until I found her. He's talking about her like he lost a pair of shoes.

"Which hospital?"

The concerned look plastered on his face falters. Then he names a local hospital.

The guys from the club have come out, forming a protective v shape around Valentine. I love them for that. They've got her back, and whatever happens here, I can count on them.

My gaze meets Kray's, and he gives me a nod and slips inside the building. He'll put in a call to our contacts at the hospital, and we'll soon find out if there's any truth in what this guy's saying.

"Why did it take you so long to find me?"

I'm proud to see Valentine stepping forward and not cowering, but it worries me too. I might be about to see her drive off with this guy, although I won't let that happen until I'm absolutely sure of him. Even then, I'll follow them home. The thought makes me shudder. I'm not ready to give up Valentine.

He pulls his brow together, giving a good impression of the concerned fiancé.

"I tried all the hospitals in the state and the police. I thought you'd turn up. It wasn't until yesterday when I was having a slice of pie at the Rosey Diner that I overheard one of the waitresses talking about it. Said there was a woman who couldn't remember anything who was staying with some bike gang."

The guys behind me shift uncomfortably at the use of the word "gang," but this guy's too stupid to notice.

"You found out yesterday? But you didn't come until this morning?"

If Valentine was my woman, I'd have ridden straight here for her. This asshole doesn't deserve her, and I'm still not convinced he's not the man who hurt her.

He shrugs. "I heard she was in safe hands."

I don't buy it. Every instinct in me tells me this asshole's lying. But Valentine takes a step toward him.

He meets her halfway, and they stare at each other. A slow smile spreads over his face that has a hint of cruelty in it.

"You really don't remember anything, do you, honey?"

The smile doesn't reach his eyes. In fact, it dissolves into a chuckle. He reaches a hand for her, and Valentine flinches.

That's all I need to spur me into action.

Valentine turns away from him, and he lays a hand on her shoulder, making her gasp as his spindly fingers dig into her skin.

"Get in the truck, now."

In one stride, I'm at her side, pulling his greasy hands off her. Pans and Jesse are with me, and they pin him against his pickup while I get Valentine the hell out of there.

"Don't make me go with him, please. Don't make me go."

She leans into me, sobbing into my chest as I usher her toward the clubhouse.

"It's okay, sweetheart." I pull her close to me, closing my arms around her. "No one's gonna make you do anything. If you want to stay here with me, then you do that."

She sobs a ragged breath, her body deflating into me.

"Do you remember him?"

"No. But the flannel shirt…" She wipes her eyes and looks up, all confusion. "When I got close enough, I could smell grease, and the panic, the fear in my stomach rose up. I don't remember him, but I think my body does."

It makes sense. If her instincts about him are right, then there's no way he's leaving here unharmed.

There're shouts behind us as the asshole struggles against my guys.

"What are you doing, asshole? I came for Abigail."

Kray comes out of the clubhouse shaking his head. "No record of an accident or a hospital stay for a man who fits his description."

I don't know how Valentine got that bump on her head or what she was doing on the highway, but it didn't happen the way he tells it.

"I didn't think so."

"What do you want us to do with him?" Pans asks.

"Tie him up in the garage. Find out who he is and who Valentine really is."

Pans nods solemnly. When there's dirty work to be done, he's the man for it. He'll get the answers that we need.

I lead Valentine into the clubhouse and away from whatever sick past tried to claim her. Her future is here, with me, and that's all that matters.

10
VALENTINE

I'm still shaking as Lyle leads me upstairs to what I've come to think of as my room. I don't remember the man in the flannel shirt, but my body remembers him.

Lyle sits on the armchair, and I crawl into his lap, letting him pat my hair and soothe me until the fear subsides.

Gina knocks on the door with a tray of food, and she stays to keep me company while Lyle goes to see how the guys are getting on. I don't know what they're doing to the man, but if he's responsible for hurting me, then I guess he deserves it.

About twenty minutes later, Lyle comes back, and Gina discreetly leaves us to it. His look is serious. I know he's got some information.

"What is it?" I sit up on the bed where I was resting.

"We found out who you are."

Nervousness jolts through me, and I'm not sure I want to know. Lyle sits next to me on the bed and takes my hand.

"Your name is Abigail Goodfellow."

"Abigail Goodfellow." My face screws up when I say it. It's a clunky name and sounds like it's straight out of the pages of the Bible. I turn the name over in my head, but it holds no meaning for me.

"You were a member of the One True Way Fellowship."

This draws a blank too, and Lyle must see my confusion.

"It's a cult," he says gently. "An extreme religious cult that is based down the coast. You were born into it."

My mind reels, and while no memories are triggered, I feel nauseated and know it must be true. If I was born into it, then the scars on my body, the whipping, must have happened there.

A sudden chill claws at my heart, making me shudder. Lyle wraps an arm protectively around me.

"A week ago, during a routine ceremony—" He scoffs at the words. "That's what the asshole called it, but it sounds more like the public humiliation of women. You were stoned and knocked unconscious." His voice threads with anger and his fist pounds the blanket. "They left you alone on the ground, unconscious and bleeding."

"Who would do that?" It's too horrible to make sense of. Who leaves an injured human being on their own?

"Assholes who don't deserve to live." Lyle fists the blankets, and I know whatever he does to the man who pretended to be my fiancé will be well deserved.

"You're lucky. You must have come to and escaped."

It sounds so horrendous. Ceremonies, being knocked unconscious. My mind's in a whirl. It's too much.

Lyle opens his mouth to speak, but I hold my hand up.

"I don't want to hear anymore."

He nods his understanding.

"It's a lot to take in, Valentine."

The use of my new name makes my head jerk up. Lyle's looking at me with true concern, and I know in my bones what I want to do.

"I never want to go back. I want to stay with you. I want to be Valentine forever."

He pulls me close, his arms wrapping protectively around me. "I was hoping you'd say that. I want you to stay, Valentine. I'll look after you and protect you always. I love you."

The words melt my heart, and I feel a lightness I've never felt before.

"I love you too."

Lyle kisses me, a slow warm kiss, and I give him everything I've got. This man found me on the side of the road, took me in, and looked after me. I owe my life to him.

He pulls back to look at me, his hands cupping my face. "I've found a doctor up the coast that deals with your condition. I've got money, Valentine. I can help you get better. I can help you remember."

He's so genuine, and my heart warms at his commitment to helping me. But if my past was so bad, do I really want to remember?

"No." I shake my head. "I don't need those memories, Lyle. My life started the moment I met you. I don't want to remember what came before."

It's the truth. This is my life now, and it will only be good memories from here on out.

"If that's what you want, baby."

"Only good memories. That's what I want."

He kisses the tears that have crept down my cheeks. But they're happy tears. I'm smiling, and Lyle's smiling back.

His hands slide around my waist and over my hips, the movement turning from comforting to something else. I feel his ownership as his hands run over my body, and I give myself freely to this man who rescued me and has shown me nothing but love. His touch feels good, and I arch my back, leaning into him and sticking my chest out.

Lyle's mouth moves down my throat, and he pulls my t-shirt off to get at my breasts.

"Let's make a good memory right now."

We move slowly, undressing each other piece by piece. His hands run over the ridges of my scars with gentle fingers, healing a wound I can't remember getting.

Lying together with our bodies pressed against each other on the bed, I feel the emptiness of my past slip away. This is my future. What came before doesn't matter, only what comes next. And Lyle is my next. He's my future, my everything.

With renewed passion, I run my hands over his body and down his hips to take his shaft in my palms. He groans as my hand moves over him, and at the same time, his fingers slide between my glistening folds.

"You're so wet."

His voice washes over me, rich and smooth and comforting—the voice of my future. His finger slides inside me, and my mind goes blank. This moment right here is all there is, our bodies moving together and Lyle's breath on my skin.

He whispers to me as his hand circles my sensitive nub.

His mouth captures my breasts, and my nipples graze against his teeth. I cry out as the pressure in my center builds under his palm. Then I'm coming as everything in the universe and everything I've ever known is forced together into one pinpoint of energy emanating from my center.

My body arches toward him as if I'm searching and Lyle is my beacon. As my pussy convulses with the orgasm, Lyle thrusts into me.

My hips buck and he grasps me tight, pulling me toward him and anchoring me to his center.

"I got you, Valentine."

Our eyes meet, and there's a current between us, an energy that's joining our souls together. With my eyes still on him, I tip my hips forward and feel myself stretch as Lyle slides deeper inside me. I want him all the way in. I want him to fill me up and never leave.

He must sense my need because he stuffs a pillow under my hips, causing him to sink deeper inside me. It's like nothing I've ever experienced. I'm sure there is nothing in my lost memories like this, so intense and so right.

My legs wrap around Lyle, and together we move, slowly at first and then faster, building a pace together as our climax grows.

I'm almost peaking when Lyle leans forward and whispers in my ear.

"I love you, Valentine. You'll always be mine."

It sends me over the edge, and I come undone completely, melting into the universe and into Lyle.

He slams into me and explodes so intensely I feel his hot cum shoot deep into my body, hitting home where I hope his seeds finds its way. I want to be tied to this man. I want our new life to start now—a future that we both create.

Afterwards, we lie in bed and talk about our new life and our dreams and plans. It's a clean slate for me. I get to choose who I am and what I want to be.

I don't know what all of that is yet, but I do know one thing: I want to be Lyle's' Valentine.

EPILOGUE

VALENTINE

Six years later…

"Can I have a cookie, Mommy?"

Hazel looks up at me with big, round eyes that no human can resist, not even her battle-worn mother.

"Okay, but this is the last one and you have to share it with your brother." She pouts at the suggestion of sharing anything with Alfie.

"But he drops half of it."

"That's what three-year-olds do, honey. But if you don't want the cookie…"

Her frown instantly turns into a smile, and I snap one of the heart-shaped chocolate chip cookies in half and give the pieces to her.

Hazel runs off to find her brother who's being bounced on Gage's knee. His high-pitched giggles fill the clubhouse and make even the hard-ass Pans smile.

I glance down at Emmy and am pleased to see she's still fast asleep in the car seat. At six months old, she still loves her naps, which buys me a bit of time to help Gina set up the clubhouse.

It's the annual Valentine's Day party. Some people may think it's unromantic to spend Valentine's Day at the club, but it's the day that me and Lyle met, and if it wasn't for him and the club's protection, I wouldn't be here.

So we alternate years with the other couples. One year we leave the kids here and go out on our own; for the next year, one of the other couples leaves their kids and we party with the club.

It's not a traditional Valentine's, but it works for us. Besides, we don't need a special day to remind us of our love.

In the six years since I met Lyle, I've never once missed my old memories.

I found out a bit more about myself. At the cult, the women were assigned work, and I worked in the kitchen. It's where I learned to handle a knife and cook bread from scratch. I'm still a mean cook and love cooking for the club.

I paint as a hobby and my work is exhibited in diners along the coast. It's something I enjoy, but my life's work is my family.

With three kids, Lyle, and the club, I'm kept busy. I love looking after the people who looked after me, who took me in when I was lost and gave me a future.

We live in a small cottage along the coast, but I spend most days at the club, helping Gina manage the place and cooking for whoever happens to be around.

The door to the club opens, and I know by the heat in my body that it's Lyle even before I turn around. I've learned to listen to my body and trust my instincts. They're never wrong.

"Hey, beautiful."

He wraps an arm around me and pulls me into a kiss. His hand slides over my rump and squeezes my butt.

"Get a room," someone calls, and I bat Lyle away playfully.

"There's a free one upstairs," Lyle murmurs.

His eyes blaze with heat. I love it when my husband looks at me like that. I glance down at the baby to check she's still asleep, but Lyle's already calling out to Gina.

"Watch the little ones for us, will ya?"

Gina gives us a broad grin as Lyle takes my hand and leads me upstairs. After six years, our passion hasn't diminished.

I love my husband. He's my safe place and my anchor. I've got six years of amazing memories with him, and I'm looking forward to a future with many more.

WHAT TO READ NEXT

PROTECTING HIS BRAT

This brat needs to be taught a lesson, and I'll be the one to discipline her...

Since retiring from the special forces, I've set up a team of elite personal security guards.

But I wasn't expecting the daughter of my first client to be such a brat.

Adrianna thinks she can play me, but she needs to be taught a lesson.

I'll be the one to take her over my knee.

She needs to learn that the only game I'm playing is for keeps.

Protecting His Brat is an OTT age-gap romance featuring an older military hero and a young curvy virgin.

Keep reading for an exclusive excerpt or visit:
mybook.to/ProtectingHisBrat

PROTECTING HIS BRAT

CHAPTER ONE

Bronn

It's an unusual house. Box-shaped rooms, jutting out at odd angles, looking like building blocks a child has stuck together.

The sun glints off the floor to ceiling windows, making me wince even behind my sunglasses.

It doesn't look homely, the hard lines making it look uncomfortable, unwelcoming, like a fortress. I should know. I've been staring at it all fucking day.

A black Mercedes waits on the driveway, the chauffeur as bored as I am.

But I'm good at waiting. I learned it in the Army, how to be still while remaining alert and how to spring into action when needed.

All good traits to be a security guard, which is about the only work I could find when I retired from the special forces.

Still, clients pay top dollar for ex-military, especially when you've been in the Green Berets.

Finally, the front door opens, and my client, Phillip Brooks, steps out.

His dark tailored suit contrasts with the sun gleaming off the white walls of the house. His wife stands in the doorway, twisting her hands nervously, looking at him with doleful eyes.

He slides an arm around her waist, and I look away as he embraces her. I feel a pang of regret. The military life never allowed me to settle down with a woman. I wonder what it's like to have someone to say goodbye to, someone to miss you when you're away.

He steps away, and she tugs on his sleeve, not wanting him to leave. Gently, he pries her hand off his arm and hurries down the stairs.

He stops next to me, and I get a whiff of bourbon and expensive aftershave.

"Don't let her leave the property."

I nod, letting him know I've understood his instructions.

My client explained the threat to me, the death threats he's been getting, his concern for his wife.

If someone had threatened my woman, I wouldn't be fucking off and leaving her alone. But it's not for me to judge. From what I understand, when you're in the oil business, like my client is, threats are a part of life.

The chauffeur holds the door open for my client, and he slides into the waiting car.

There's a wrought iron gate at the entrance to the property, and I scan the area around it, making sure there's nothing suspect before we open the gates.

As the car circles around the drive, I catch movement on the road.

My skin prickles, and I'm instantly on high alert. A black car is driving slowly down the road, too slow to be going straight past.

I jog in front of the Merc, holding my hand out to stop them. My client ducks down in the back seat, protecting himself from whatever threat this might be.

The black car comes to a stop outside the gate. It's got tinted windows, so I can't see who's inside.

Every fiber of my body is alert, my blood thumping, ready to meet the threat. I pull my piece and aim it at the car, keeping my hand steady.

The back door of the car opens, and I train my gun on whatever's going to come out of there. I won't be the first to fire, but if someone attacks, I won't hesitate to shoot.

There's the flutter of bright fabric, a flash of tanned leg, and a young woman slides out of the backseat. She's wearing a short, floaty dress that comes halfway up her thick thighs. It dips at the front, displaying a full cleavage of soft breast.

My mouth waters, and there's a twitch in my pants. If this is how my clients' enemies attack, then I'm screwed.

She can't be a day over twenty, but my dick doesn't seem to mind the age gap.

The woman shuts the door behind her and saunters over to the gate.

She slides her large designer glasses down her nose and peers at me over the rim, unimpressed by the gun I've got pointed at her.

"If this is the welcome I get, I would have stayed away." Her voice is as pouty as her look. Sassy and sharp.

I've been trained to encounter all kinds of enemies but not an entitled brat with a sticky pink pout and a mane of golden hair clasping an overnight bag to her plus-sized chest.

A car door slams behind me.

"Put the gun down, Bronn."

I slowly lower my piece, but I can't tear my eyes away from the woman. She wraps both hands around the iron bars and leans forward rattling the gate.

"Open the gate, Daddy."

Her voice is whiny and petulant, like an overgrown toddler. Like a spoiled brat who needs some discipline.

My client strides forward, irritation in his voice. "You're supposed to be at college."

The woman tears one hand off the gate and swipes at her golden hair. "It was boring."

"Did you get kicked out?" My client's voice is clipped, his anger not quite disguised.

The woman gives him a sweet smile.

"I wanted to be here with you instead."

My client harumphs and pushes the code for the gate. It swings open, and the woman sashays through.

"I've got a business trip. You can stay here with your mother."

"Oh, great," mutters the woman, and even though I can't see behind her glasses, I'm sure she's rolling her eyes. If any kid of mine spoke about my wife like that, I'd tan their hide. But her father doesn't react.

"Don't give your mother any trouble," he barks at her.

"I'll be back in ten days. You stay inside these gates and I'll deal with you when I get back."

The daughter does a slow twirl as if checking out her surroundings. Her eyes rest on me, and my body tenses as she looks me up and down.

"Who's the heavy?" she asks her father as if I'm not there.

"I'm Bronn."

Both the woman and her father look at me in surprise. To them, I'm the hired help, the silent security guard. But this brat needs to learn some respect. If her father isn't teaching her ,then I will.

She slides the sunglasses onto her head, showing off her large brown eyes. There's a mischievous look in them as she saunters toward me.

"Hello, Bronn."

My cock lengthens despite myself. I shift uncomfortably, clasping my hands in front of my body, hiding what's going on in my pants.

"I'm Adrianna."

From a distance, she was beautiful, but up close, she takes my breath away. I literally can't breathe as I stare at her, transfixed by her dark, playful eyes.

Heat sweeps over me, and I feel unbalanced. A surge of protectiveness rushes through me, and one thought bangs into my brain.

Mine.

"Bronn's here to protect you and your mother. Do exactly as he says and don't do anything stupid."

She's so close to me I can smell her cherry-flavored lip balm and expensive floral soap.

"Oh. I'll do exactly what you tell me to do," she murmurs so only I can hear.

My gaze flicks to her lips, so full, so pouty—just the right size for my cock.

Then she flicks her hair and flounces up the driveway.

I am so fucked.

Keep reading at: mybook.to/ProtectingHisBrat

GET YOUR FREE BOOK

Sign up to the Sadie King mailing list for a FREE book! You'll be the first to hear about exclusive offers, bonus content and all the news from Sadie King.

I see her on stage, and I know she'll be mine...

The Biker's Private Dancer is an age gap, MC-lite short and steamy instalove romance featuring an OTT possessive biker and a curvy girl with a secret.

The Biker's Private Dancer is a bonus book in the Underground Crows MC series available exclusively to Sadie King email subscribers.

To claim your free copy visit:
www.authorsadieking.com/free

BOOKS BY SADIE KING

Sunset Coast

Underground Crows MC

Sunset Security

Men of the Sea

The Thief's Lover

The Henchman's Obsession

The Hitman's Redemption

Wild Heart Mountain

Mountain Heroes

Military Heroes

Wild Riders MC

Maple Springs

Men of Maple Mountain

All the Single Dads

Candy's Café

Small Town Sisters

Kings County

Kings of Fire

King's Cops

For a full list of titles check out the Sadie King website

www.authorsadieking.com

ABOUT THE AUTHOR

Sadie King is a USA Today Best Selling Author of short instalove romance.

She lives in New Zealand with her ex-military husband and raucous young son.

When she's not writing she loves catching waves with her son, running along the beach, and good wine, preferably drunk with a book in hand.

Keep in touch when you sign up for her newsletter. You'll even snag yourself a free short romance! www.authorsadieking.com/free

www.ingramcontent.com/pod-product-compliance
Ingram Content Group UK Ltd.
Pitfield, Milton Keynes, MK11 3LW, UK
UKHW040012200726
13854UKWH00001B/165

9 798215 105504